KEEP ON MOVING

BOOK 1

Tiny Little Steps

WRITTEN AND ILLUSTRATED BY

STEFFANI SEVEN

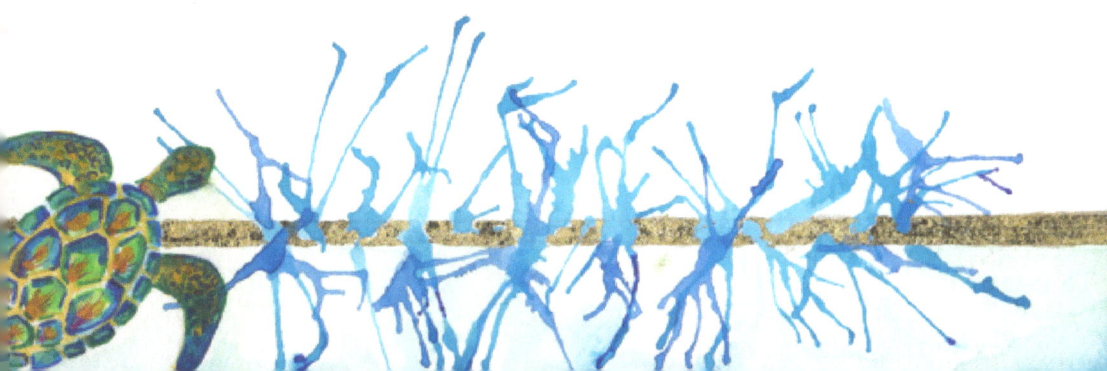

This book is dedicated as
a legacy to my three sons
David, Israel and Shaebron.

One starry summer night, Mummy Turtle swam from home in the middle of the deep turquoise ocean and headed to Lotus Island.

The moon was high, full and shone a beautiful light on the shore where Mummy Turtle would finally come to nest.

But Mommy Turtle had a few more miles to cover. She was already exhausted by her long journey and sometimes felt like giving up. Still, the thought of losing her precious cargo gave her more strength and determination.

She kept on Moving.

Finally, her fins touched the sparkling sand. Her heavy shell and precious package made it very difficult for her to move through the thick sand, especially since she was hungry and tired. But she knew she had to keep on moving.

She began to make a comfortable nest, a hole with the perfect depth and width to create the ideal temperature. It was time to bury her treasure. She dug and dug as she knew she had to keep on moving.

One by one, Mommy Turtle released her soft eggs into the cozy nest. This was a bitter-sweet moment since she knew she would have to leave and may never see her babies. Her babies may never see their mother. She could no longer stay and had no choice but to keep on moving.

She covered her precious eggs with the jeweled sand and sang them a lullaby.

"Keep on moving.
Gotta keep on moving.
Don't be afraid of losing.
The beat of life keeps grooving.
Get up and keep on moving."

Then off she went.

One early morning as the warm sun woke up, something magical happened. The baby turtles began to peek their tiny heads through the sand. They heard their mother's voice as the waves splashed on the shore. It was the same song she never stopped singing. They excitedly began to make their way to the music from the water. This gave

them the courage to just keep on moving. Across the glistening sand where Mummy Turtle once traveled, they "wibbled and wabbled" one tiny step at a time with the beat of the song in their hearts. They have finally begun the cycle of a never-ending journey, as someday at least one of the baby turtles would make her way back to Lotus Island.

Just like Mummy Turtle, we all have something unique and precious carrying around in our soul and spirit.

We sometimes get tired and discouraged as we journey through life. There are times we have to stop, take a break, and even sometimes make significant and unforeseen changes.

Change is inevitable, and sometimes when we don't change, life changes.

We should never forget that we are loaded with an abundance of possibilities, potential and dreams to fulfill. We can only accomplish them if we at least try, one tiny little step at a time.

We just have to keep on moving.

"Wibble Wabble"
Acrylic on Canvas Collage.
80cm x100cm
Acrylic paint, resin, mother of pearl, driftwood, swarovski crystals and goldleaf

This is the first piece to be added to her online Vernissage. She awaits her official art exhibition where all her works will be ripe and ready to be presented.

Jamaican born and raised Steffani Seven is a professional singer, songwriter, recording artist, dancer, jewelry designer, goldsmith, actress, author and illustrator. Steffani has completed nine years of studies at the Edna Manley College of the Visual and Performing Arts in Kingston Jamaica. She holds a Bachelor of Fine Arts Degree in Jewellery Design and a Diploma in Dance Theatre and Production. She has performed as a singer, actress and dancer in the Broadway Musical "The Lion King" where she was a cast member for approximately 7 years. She is presently enrolled in the University of Mataphysics to obtain her Doctorate in Metaphysical studies.

This book Keep on Moving: Tiny Little Steps is the first of her series of short stories that will be available.

Steffani hopes to use her influence to protect nature and our environment.

For more information on her projects , please visit www.steffaniseven.com

www.ingramcontent.com/pod-product-compliance
Lightning Source LLC
LaVergne TN
LVHW052303100826
845147LV00001B/129

* 9 7 8 1 7 3 7 0 2 0 5 0 9 *